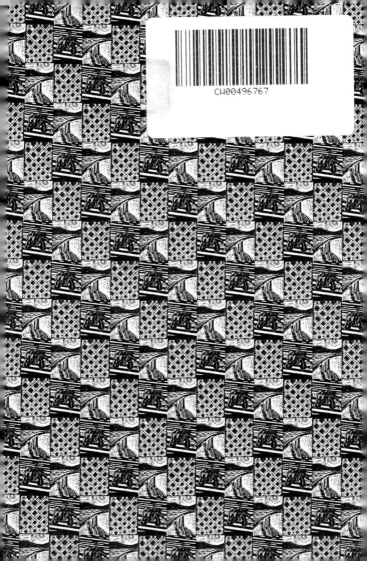

CW00496767

All rights reserved
Published by Bradawl Books 2022
Designed by Vicky Fullick, The Type Shed
Printed by Swallowtail Print
www.bradawlbooks.com
Instagram: threewordsthreestories

THREE WORDS THREE STORIES

GRAPES
CATTLE-GRID
NECKLACE

BOOK ONE

The Dam 1962

Anna Fairbank

After the speeches and ribbon cutting, the mayor and his party were invited to view the turbines. The procession of local worthies, professionals connected with the project, other guests and families started to make their way across the top of the dam. The photographer kept close to the main party. He had already shot two rolls of film but was in no hurry to get back to the office. He was hoping for good pictures in the powerhouse. The young engineer and his wife had been seated at the back and were among the last to leave the temporary platform. Their three-year-old daughter wore a white dress and kept stopping to pick up small pieces of gravel from the new tarmac. She carried a child-sized handbag in the crook of her elbow in perfect imitation of her mother and she wore a bracelet around her plump wrist and a string of plastic beads around her neck not dissimilar to her mother's pearls.

The engineer, tall and brisk with nervous movements and a suit designed for someone shorter and fatter, wanted to be close enough to the mayor to field questions about design, capacity and so on – to make it clear to everyone that, despite the impression given by the opening address, he was the man responsible for the project and his boss knew precious little about it. He hoped to catch up with him once they were walking along the dam.

It was an unusually bright day. Hot for June

and very still. The empty moorland around the reservoir soaked up sunshine the way it had soaked up rain for the last month. Heavy, passive, sponge like, it dozed and brooded. Site visits in the first winter had been deep in mud. Mud ramps, mud tracks, excavators stuck in mud and then for a year and a half he'd watched the huge concrete wave rising up across the valley exactly as he'd drawn it. And then the flood. The slow filling as a glistening stream swelled into a deep sullen lake.

The engineer's wife played her part as diligently as she did everything. She was lucky to have married a man with a profession and she admired him despite his awkwardness. She was unaware of ever putting herself first. She only cared so meticulously for her appearance: her hair, her make up, her neat, well-chosen clothes, to ensure she didn't let him down and only flirted charmingly, if a little coolly, with his boss to further his career. She worried she might say or do the wrong thing. So, though poised, was never quite relaxed. The engineer was proud of her and she was bringing up their daughter to play her part too. To speak nicely when spoken to. To be always pretty and pleasing. To let strange gentlemen pinch her cheeks. Never to scowl or scream or bite. The engineer's wife had a few grapes in her handbag and now and then inconspicuously slipped off one of her white gloves, reached into her bag and held out a shiny green jewel to the little girl.

Say please.

Say thank you.

Good girl. Walk nicely.

But it was too much to expect of a three-year-old. They had been out in the sun for more than an hour and movement down the dam was slow. Even a good little girl can get bored and tired. The engineer's wife looked out for points of interest, but the dam was dull for the child who began to moan that she wanted to go home now. She tugged at her mother's smart skirt and asked to be carried and then took off her bracelet and dropped it and then pulled at her necklace, trying to get it off, until it broke and pale pink beads rolled across the concrete under the feet of important people. As her face started to pucker her father picked her up, so for a few paces, she had a view over the parapet at the broad, flat, shining water. But then he noticed the mayor not far ahead and put her down again muttering to his wife.

Try and keep her happy, darling.

The photographer had taken three shots of the engineer's wife's legs which were smooth and shapely in their nylon sheaths. And one of the back of her neck. He enjoyed watching her slip off her glove and her hand going into her bag and reappearing with yet another perfect grape. Her fingers were quick and elegant, her nails shaped and polished like slim shells. She had slightly uneven teeth. He had lost all interest in the opening of the dam or the mayor's connections. The heat was getting to him. His best suit was thick but none of the men had taken off their jackets.

The three-year-old walked stolidly beside her mother, trying to keep her father in sight and bravely not crying about her beads. But when she thought of them rolling away and not being allowed to pick them up it was hard not to wail. She seemed to be on an endless path. There were people walking and talking and there was sky and concrete and sun bouncing off everything into her eyes. It was a big wall holding back water and Daddy had made it. But she couldn't see the water. To one side of the path was a metal grill over a drainage channel but there was no water in it. It was a special day and she wanted to be at home sitting under the table, and she wanted to see the water, and her beads had all gone. She started sobbing and when her mother picked her up she didn't stop but cried louder.

Want to go home.

Go home.

Mumamamamaa.

Beads gone. All gone.

Need to go.

MUMUMUMUMUMAA.

The engineer's wife was resourceful and kind and since there were no more grapes she quickly took off her pearls and fastened them around her daughter's neck.

You can wear Mummy's pretty beads.

Say thank you.

Be careful with them.

Good girl. Hang on. Won't be long now.

And still the procession of over-dressed people shuffled across the curved white dam in the sunshine, like a wedding party. It was an inspiring sight: colourful hats and dresses and the clean lines of modern engineering; the promise of a controlled water supply and electricity for the region. The little girl snuggled into her mother's neck and fiddled reverently with the pearls.

Towards the middle of the dam a short section of fenced metal walkway crossed one of the overflow outfalls before reaching the entrance to the internal stairs leading down to the powerhouse. Water emerged from a hidden channel, twenty feet below, and cascaded down the bright concrete cliff. People stopped moving as some wanted to look and others hesitated to walk across the open metal grill with so much space beneath their feet. The mayor's wife's stiletto heel stuck in a hole and there was much amusement as an elderly councillor knelt in front of her trying to release it. The mayor's wife was wearing a fur coat and, although well known for her generosity (particularly to local children's homes), was too hot to enjoy jokes at her expense. She appeared to snap at her spouse and dabbed at perspiration running down the sides of her powdered face with a tiny handkerchief. But once the heel was free she made a success of removing her other shoe with a flourish and waving the exquisite items in the faces of the crowd and laughing in her most attractive way.

Careful ladies! We are walking over a cunningly

designed trap!

The engineer would have responded with a clever quip, if he'd been close enough to be heard without shouting. He tried to catch up with the mayor's group by overtaking slow movers but it took him a few minutes. It was his first major job. He hoped it would be the first of many.

With well-mannered persistence (as he supposed) he at last managed to position himself to one side and slightly behind the mayor who was discussing costs with a contractor. He listened politely, even chuckled at the right moment and was rewarded with a glance which seemed to approve his participation. But he must have misread the look, because his very apposite remark about the structure was ignored, and the two men turned and walked ahead soon after, leaving no space for him to join them. His boss was one of the people he had pushed past. It was altogether very uncomfortable.

The child struggled in her mother's arms and

insisted on being put down. The metal walkway was the most interesting place with a view through railings to the side and down through the floor which was like a cattle-grid but with much narrower gaps. Her mother held her hand tightly and kept her away from the railings through which a three-year-old could just possibly have squeezed.

Walk carefully. Don't lose your shoe.

It seemed a silly idea that she would let her shoe come off and that it could go down a small hole. She wanted to see if her shoe could go through. Or her handbag. She lined them up but both were too big.

Careful with the necklace.

The photographer took a few more photographs of the dam. The light was perfect and the crisp concrete lines looked sensational. He had taken a quick snap of the mayor's wife magnificently waving her stilettos and some of the engineer's wife looking out across the moors while holding the hand of her daughter. The pair made a good picture. If only the little girl would stand straight instead of twisting and bending. Now she had slipped her mother's hand and was fiddling with something. The mother had lovely cheekbones. He thought he had about another ten shots before he needed to change his film.

The child was quiet now, fascinated by the metal pattern of the walkway and the roaring water far below. And by the terrible idea of Mummy's necklace falling through one, into the other. Could that happen? She imagined holding it by one end so it hung down straight over a hole … and letting go. She wouldn't do that. She felt the clasp. If it just came undone, would the necklace fall across the grid? And if she held both ends and stretched it out as wide as it could go and then dropped it? Surely that would be OK?

The photographer was watching through his lens and saw it all but even he wasn't close enough or quick enough to stop it and the engineer rejoined his wife and child just in time to see the necklace fall. It lay diagonally across the grid for a moment with just the clasp and two or three beads hanging down a slit but then, one by one, the next pearls slid after them and once a third of the necklace was out of sight the rest rolled sideways and shifted and suddenly there was a flicker of smooth shiny movement like a slowworm, or like teeth glimpsed in a smile and the necklace disappeared and fell into the roaring water.

The child stared after it and after a few seconds' frozen silence started screaming. She was comforted brusquely by her shocked mother.

You've lost Mummy's necklace! Why did you do that? You silly girl.

She couldn't explain but cried louder and as people crowded around to see what had happened there were raised eyebrows and comments on the foolishness of letting a child wear expensive jewellery.

Pearls!

A child that age!

The engineer's wife wiped her daughter's face then managed a brave smile.

Really, it's nothing … No, they weren't real pearls. Artificial. It's really nothing to worry about.

Of course the engineer could only afford imitation pearls for his wife but she had so enjoyed wearing them, walking along the dam in her best clothes. She was mortified to have to admit they weren't real in front of so many important people. The matching earrings burned in her ears. Their daughter was still wailing and she couldn't quieten her, and her husband was losing his chance of talking about the project. She was sure she had damaged his prospects.

But her confusion and embarrassment about her loss were so graceful, and the little girl so upset, that the effect was an increase of sympathy, rather than the reverse, towards the gawky but actually rather handsome young man some had thought unpleasantly pushy up to that point, and who was now carrying his daughter and dabbing her eyes, pointing out where Daddy did his measuring and calculating, and where there used to be a little house which was now deep under the water. The mayor even came up and shook his hand and congratulated him on his work. He said it was a pleasure to meet a young man starting his professional life with such success and he hoped to meet him again.

The photographer captured the moment. It made a good picture; the corpulent mayor clasps the hand of the engineer, tall and eager in profile, who awkwardly holds his little daughter with his other arm, her white dress against his dark suit, while behind him is his smiling wife, whose quiet style, obvious pride in her husband and beguiling curves as she lifts a hand to her hair ensured that the photograph appeared on the front page of the local paper.

The little girl was fretful then sick in the car on the way home and afterwards only remembered too much brightness and the horror of beads falling through a grill into thundering water, but her parents looked back on it as the splendid day the engineer first made his mark.

Shasu

Helen Wright

He was holding something up to my face.
A shard of silver pinched between his dusty
fingers, his nails yellow, horn-like, curling round
his finger tips, his voice cracked and urgent.
Even I, with my freshly learnt ear, could tell
that his Arabic was heavily accented. Market
sellers' cries echoed off the ancient stone walls
of the souk. Somewhere I could hear the call to
prayer. Romantic. Exotic. My new love. The East.

He said it again, his tongue pushing against a few remaining stubs of teeth. Deep in his lined face were two sapphire eyes, clear and sharp and holding me in their gaze. He barked again – something guttural, but in German this time.

'Aussehen. Deine Zukunft. Siehst Frau?'

I searched my schoolgirl German and for a moment glimpsed myself uniformed, at a scratched, ink-stained desk, ivy growing up stone mullioned windows, the clipped emerald lawns, and the dreams of a glorious future. The man nodded, held up a magnifying glass and thrust his other hand up to my face.

Adam pulled at my sleeve. 'Move on, my love. These fellows just want one thing, your lovely American dollars.'

I shrugged him off.

'I want to see,' I said, 'It doesn't cost to look.'

I smelt sweet paprika burning into lamb's flesh from the stall next door.

'Siehst Frau.'

I took the magnifying glass and held it up,

focusing on the silver fleck pinched between the man's thumb and forefinger. I could see lines of dirt mapping out his finger-print, and one of his nails had a crack running down to the wick.

'What?' I laughed, embarrassed, 'What is it?'

His eyes searched mine and he whispered 'Sehen Sie.'

Then I saw it. A pin. A silver pin held tight and firm and remarkably still for such an ancient man. I moved the glass closer and leaned forward slightly allowing a shaft of light to fall on the glimmering object.

Carved in beautiful detail was a bunch of grapes sitting in front of a half-filled champagne glass. An intricate tracery of veins could be seen on the leaves and curling tendrils of the vine. The top of the flute was encircled with engraved fretwork like crenellations on a medieval castle. The glasses were identical to the ones Adam and I had just chosen for our wedding party.

The silver-work was exquisite. I looked again at the man. Who was he? From my years of trading jewels I had taught my eye to see such tiny detail, but many would be blind to the skill of it.

'It is beautiful,' I said. 'Schön. Das ist dein Arbeit?'

He nodded, withdrew his hand for a moment, then returned it to its station in front of my face. I felt Adam's breath on my neck. 'My love! Mother is expecting us!'

I leaned in once more. This time another tiny sculpture carved out of the few molecules of silver. A beautiful necklace resting on an elegant neck I knew to be my own. Its fine links embellished with clusters of pearl, the pendant a twisted love-link weighting the chain down over the collar bone. Involuntarily my hand rose to my neck and held the self same love-link. The man's eyes widened. He nodded.

Adam shifted at my side.

'You cannot be seen trading with a gypsy, my love. A man of the desert. A man not fit to clean your shoes.'

I looked at Adam. A bead of sweat coalesced

on his temple and made its way down the side of his face. His disgust at the stranger surprised me.

'Hier.' The old man held out a third piece of silver. I raised the magnifying glass and adjusted it. I could not make out the image. Some strong bars, like a cattle-grid! I hadn't seen one of those for over a year, since my voyage began. The bars that imprisoned the livestock while giving the illusion of an open gate. I looked into the old man's eyes. He adjusted the pin in his hand and I looked again.

This time the bars were arranged vertically. The sun moved, light flooded the stall and I saw that clasped round two of the bars was a pair of hands, one wearing my own bespoke engagement ring. Behind, in the shadow, my face, my mournful face staring out into the sunlight. I gasped. The man nodded. I turned to Adam.

'Darling – you must see this. The work is exquisite.'

But when I turned back the old man had gone.

Lost And Found

Val Rutt

Grief has altered my perception of time and in the minutes it takes to boil a kettle I relive a day from 50 years ago.

'Don't worry darling.'

'It's all right Mummy, I can do it.'

I am standing behind my mother in the back of our pewter-grey Humber Hawk, trying to re-clasp her necklace, which I have undone. I am struggling with it; my thumbnail keeps slipping off the catch, but I am sure that the combination of skill and luck I need will align at any moment.

I had wriggled my way off the back seat to be near my mother, to stand with my arms around her neck, resting my cheek against hers. She smelled of the baked fruit pie still warm in the picnic basket, hairspray and toothpaste. In response to my father's curt, 'Sit down Audrey', I said that my mother's necklace was not fastened properly – this was untrue, I was unfastening it as I spoke; inventing the excuse as a reason to defy him. I set about re-clasping the pearls, adopting an air of solicitous attention to the task that made me feel grown up. Father drove us through country lanes of high hedges and flickering light while I focused on the clasp, my wrists resting on the maroon leather bench-seat either side of Mother's lowered head. I was balanced precariously, glancing up when I felt nauseous, then back down to concentrate on my stiffening fingers as they tried to perform this task that I had had no idea could be so difficult.

And then my brother reached out and nudged my shoulder and began a low sound, deep in his throat,

'Whurrr,' he droned.

'Not now, John,' I said flicking my elbow at him, 'Can't you see I'm busy?'

The game he was starting had been a favourite, though we never played it again after that day. We had chanced upon the fun of it in the midst of a quarrel. John had been bellowing a song in my face and I had pummelled his chest with the heels of my palms to make him stop. The wonderful, absurd vibrato that ensued made us laugh, the fight forgotten. 'Thumpalong' we called it and it became a guess-that-tune game where one of us would drone while the other beat a rhythm on their sternum. That day, in the car, John's timing was off and I was contemptuous. I couldn't play thumpalong now, couldn't he see that Mummy needed me to help her with her necklace? But John, who had been watching the road over father's shoulder, saw a cattle-grid – and a unique opportunity for thumpalong fast approaching. Just as the clasp caught, John and the car made the Gatling-gun noise. I lost my balance and yanked on the necklace which snapped at my mother's throat sending pearls flying. As our father brought us to a stop, I held up one end of the necklace and the remaining pearls slid from their thread and spilled softly into my mother's lap.

While we searched the car for scattered pearls my father told me that the necklace was an heirloom and had belonged to his mother and I should not have been playing with it.

'I wasn't playing,' I countered, but he cut me off, 'I don't want to hear it, Audrey.'

His disapproval stung and on impulse I said,

'It's John's fault – he jogged me!'

John, on his hands and knees in the back of the car, looked up and glared at me open-mouthed. Before he could protest, Father said,

'If you had sat down as you had been told Audrey, it would not have happened.'

Later, after a supper that I was unable to eat for weeping, John pushed past me on the stairs and called me a liar and a cry-baby.

In the back of the car a few months later and while retrieving coins that had slipped from the pocket of his shorts, John had pried his hands into the dusty gap where the backrest joined the seat and, after recovering his shilling and sixpence, felt a tiny ball roll beneath his fingers. He had been pleased with his find but my father had taken the lost pearl solemnly from John's palm and frowned at me. By then, the necklace had been restrung and it was too late to include this lost one. My mother's forgiveness had been generous and absolute, 'Please don't fret darling,' she had said, 'Far worse things happen.' But the pearls were a reminder of my shabby behaviour and brought unwelcome feelings. Whenever my mother wore them, my stomach took a dive at the sight of them.

John died five months ago. He was 62 and his death was sudden and a shock. I had just arrived at the care home where our mother now lives, when John's wife Marilyn called me from the ambulance. John had collapsed as he opened the front door that morning. Instead of stepping over the threshold into the day, he had sunk to his knees and fallen head first onto the steps. We agreed that I would wait for more news before I told mother. And so I sat with her, making conversation, trying not to let my anxiety show.

The next day, I visited John in the Intensive Care Unit, bringing with me a bag of grapes bought from the vendor at Vauxhall station. In the ICU family waiting room, I used the phone as instructed and a nurse came, introduced heself as Nurse Kutani, and escorted me to John's bedside. His eyes were closed and I was grateful that he was not witness to my dismayed reckoning of the tubes going in and out of him. John's face was grey and sagging; his eyes were bruised from the fall and a split across his brow was pulled together with steri-strips.

I sat down and took the grapes from my bag and held them out to nurse Kutani, nodding towards the nil-by-mouth sign at John's head.

'Sorry, I wasn't thinking.'

'Oh, I think it'll be OK, we're just waiting for the consultant to confirm that he's not going to theatre.'

'Oh?'

'Has John's wife spoken to you?'

John opened his eyes and Nurse Kutani turned her attention to him.

'Look, your sister is here to see you.' She reached out for the grapes.

'Let me wash these.'

I touched the back of John's hand, careful of the canula.

'Hi Aud, you brought me grapes, that's nice.'

'How are you feeling?' I regretted the question but it was out.

'I think I'm in trouble, Aud.'

'I'm sure it's – '

'I've got a bad feeling about it.'

'Well, you're bound to, it's such a shock.'

'Yeah. Sorry about that. How's Mum?'

'She's fine, well, she doesn't know – we thought we'd wait for more news.'

He said,

'Do you mind taking a look at my feet?'

I got up and moved to the end of the bed and lifted the sheet.

'They still there?'

'Shall I rub them for you?'

'Ah, you don't want to do that – '

But I did – I wanted to do something, anything for him. I dragged the chair to the end of the bed. John's feet were puffy and blue, I began to massage them and Nurse Kutani returned with the grapes, wet now but still musty, in a grey cardboard bowl.

'After Mr. Phillips has seen you,' pointing to the grapes, then, 'Do you want some crushed ice?'

As she brought a paper cone to his lips, she smiled at me,

'Spa treatments, that's so nice.'

I swept my palms in circles across John's feet and he closed his eyes. After a while he said,

'Remember Dad's story? Longbones is Dead?'

'Yes, how could I forget that?'

'My eyeballs feel like a couple of peeled grapes.' he exhaled, a substitute for laughter.

When John was 14 and I was 12 we hosted a Halloween party – no trick-or-treat back then, but games and our father telling a ghost story in a darkened room, an upward-pointing torch in his lap. We had each invited three friends and after tea, hair damp from apple bobbing, we sat cross-legged in a semi-circle around father. He had things hidden beneath a blanket and he fussed with these for a few minutes before signalling to mother, who turned out the light as he turned on the torch. The beam threw a shadow of his elongated head up the wall and across the ceiling. He spoke in a slow, rasping voice,

'Old Longbones, the warrior brave and true,

has died on the battlefield and I bring to you news of his death!'

There were jeers and giggles,

'What's that? You don't believe me? Hold out your hands!'

Father reached beneath the blanket and passed a bowl of lukewarm, oily spaghetti round the circle, 'Here are Boney's guts' he growled and as each of us dipped our fingers into the gloop we could not see, there were groans, squeals and shouts of laughter. Next came Boney's ear in the form of a dried apricot, followed by Boney's heart which, I remember, was slippery, warm and pulsating.

'And here are his eye-balls,' rasped my father placing two peeled grapes into the upturned palm of Lucy Myers who, near hysterical from her repulsion at the oozing guts and pumping heart, screamed and flung them into the darkness. When the laughter and the recriminations abated, my father continued, passing two more peeled grapes in the opposite direction, directly into the steady hands of my brother's best friend, Martin Cleveland.

'Ha!' John quipped, 'Good job Boney had four eyes!'

I look up from John's feet and despite the peaks and troughs on the screen he is lost to me and I feel compelled to give his foot a squeeze. He opens his eyes.

'Remember that other game we used to play,' I say, 'That juddering noise you made while I thumped your chest? We called it *thumpalong*?'

He gazes at me, the blue eyes of his boyhood unchanged in the mask of his face.

'I think it'd be unfair to Nurse Kutani if we started doing that, Aud.'

John died that night and in the morning I made my dreadful journey to the care home carrying the news of his death to our mother. John's joke about being unfair to Nurse Kutani was the focus of that first, shocked grief. As I walked, I railed bitterly against death; the despot King of Unfair. It was not fair to John, nor was it fair to Marilyn, nor their daughters, one expecting his first grandchild. I halt on the pavement struck by a wave of self-pity – it is not fair to me. He is my brother I want to shout, my only brother. And then comes another blow, for what can be more unfair than a mother outliving her son? She is ninety and yet she will mourn the loss of him as if he has died in infancy and her work of raising him is not done.

Months of grieving pass. The memories of childhood that John recalled for us in the hospital haunt me. I wait for the kettle, for the bus, for sleep – and I inhabit a time when we had two parents and we, as siblings, were a couple. John and Audrey, Audrey and John. We climb trees and build sandcastles, we wrestle and we run, we play hours of Yahtzee on rainy days. We tease, we mock, we boast, we apologize. I hear our names called out together through the door-ways and open windows of our childhood – John! Audrey! Shouted out across fields and beaches – Audrey! John! Time for tea! Time for bed! I can see our names written, first one then the other, on birthday and Christmas cards to our parents and grandparents. Lots of love and kisses, John and Audrey, lots of love, Audrey and John xx

I relive the day I broke our mother's pearls in crystal clarity and then, as the water boils I rouse myself to lift the kettle and I think of the necklace tucked away in the bottom drawer of my desk. I take my tea and get out the box and sit awhile gazing at the string of pearls. After our father died, when Mother gave them to me, I had been reluctant to take them. I thought John should have them – they had been passed from our father's mother to her son's wife and I argued that there was a precedent there and that Marilyn would be more likely to wear them than me. I made a good case, but John insisted I keep them.

I lift the pearls and pass them through my fingers. I am 50 years from the child who broke them but I can feel the shock of them flying apart and remember my father's disappointment that they were incomplete when restrung. The necklace does not please me – I think of each pearl as bereft, sitting self-consciously beside the wrong neighbour.

I hold the necklace at arms' length trying to get some perspective and all at once things shift. There is a break in the clouds, autumn sunshine drenches my desk and as I turn the necklace the pearls are transformed. I notice their translucent beauty, their radiant creaminess, the sense of each pearl being a tiny perfect planet.

For the first time in months, my thoughts begin running forwards. It occurs to me that when John's grandchild is born I will give the necklace to my niece. I imagine Rebecca opening the box and I know she will value them – not just for their beauty but for how they serve in remembrance of her father. Her baby will come soon and I want to get the pearls ready for her.

I buff them to a shine with a soft cloth and plan to display them as a jeweller would. I prise the insert from the box, eager to lay a loop of pearls against the black velvet – and there, in the hidden-space beneath, the lost pearl rolls against my fingers. I trap it and hold it up to the light.

'Look what I've found!' an echo of John's voice, excited and pleased, comes back to me and with it, somehow, a sense that I am not broken beyond repair. John is dead and life is not the same – months of grieving have altered me – but I am recovering. I cherish memories, but do not long for the lost companion of my childhood. I miss him, but I am no longer tormented by his absence. Look what I've found, I think, as I hold the lone pearl to the light and wonder at its full-moon perfection.